SECOND ROBIN

SECOND ROBIN

PART II

Rajesh Dutta

PARTRIDGE
A Penguin Random House Company

To order additional copies of this book, contact
Partridge India
000 800 10062 62
orders.india@partridgepublishing.com

www.partridgepublishing.com/india

CONTENTS

Dedicated to the memory of YD
As God required it….

PROLOGUE

City of Constantia

Since Ray thought that danger flickered over the little nest of the three robin chicks in the hedge outside the kitchen, he took them out and put them in an unused window covered on the outside with a broad wire net so that it became like a large but flat rectangular cage, through which the mother and father birds fed them.

Over time the fuss of feathers sorted out into beautifully festooned wings and frilled heads. But this dressing of the drab window in robin fashion ended one day when in a severe attack, a falcon injured the first one, causing it to die later. Ray became desperate to save the other two. He took *the second one* out into the unappeased late morning breeze of the Fairy Dale. The little bird fluffed up and lifted itself out of his fingers into waves of bright sunlight for a few seconds and then as quickly yielded to a moderately humble descent.

It was not entirely a futile attempt. What happened after the second attempt was predictable. The feral scream of a sentinel bird ripped through the seemingly tamed Dale as a pair of talons unfastened themselves from a high perch somewhere and Ray experienced, for the first time, an intrepid falcon's flash of audacity. The little creature disappeared from his hand like a ghost vanishing from an illusion.

He came out crashing through waves and waves of shock and ran in a blind, drunken stampede after the wanton blur of debauchery, his mouth articulating an ancient cry. The Fairy Dale can turn into an alien ground at such times and stretched out immediately into parts Ray feared to venture into. Trees that stood estranged from the general vegetation of the landscape. Bushes insubordinate to the rules of the plant kingdom.

A falcon's leisure is worth beholding. In the comfort of the top branch of one such tree, it held down the inert little body and soon soft downy feathers floated about idly like affluence going through slow destruction. For each one of the feathers coming down, he threw up a stone but his vehement antagonism was no match to the feathery patchwork forming fast on the ground around him and he must have realized that they were the only thing he could recover. He withdrew like a tranqulised conclusion.

1

The picturesque Fairy Dale matches the ornate façade of Constantia. The L'art rises over the bund and the motionless lake on one side and on the other, the webbed wood, its roots rinsed by the amnesiac river. The wind is the only correspondent between the khajoor fronds for miles across this landscape when the school is closed for the vacations. Besides a general under-song of the dead in the rustling brown leaves, there is a shuffling of nothingness in the third house at the corner of the compound beyond the white gate.

The weather is no romancer here. During the summers the shuffling is joined by a menacing heatwave. Rumour is that a conference materializes between two wrecks of time. In an orgy of dust, a father and son have been seen holding hysterical ceremony in the courtyard. During the rains weightless drops remain suspended for hours like snapshots drowning in suffocating memories. In the winters the cry of the falcons becomes shriller against the cultic sun, dilating into a tormenting eye over the courtyard.

'It is a haunted house.' Every new occupant feels and moves soon to another house somewhere else in Constantia's lap. The house lies undisturbed and those who live around it, perpetuate the unfinished legend of Bonny and Yogesh, themselves craving to bring it to an end but doomed not to. The delirious spirits relive the entire course of their serpentine tale from the beginning to the end. Eternity does not restrain them. Death cannot touch them. And blood vanishes from the countenance of those who are still alive but involved in this tale.

2

Yogesh divided wind, scattered light, twisted narrow shades into wide swathes of hate, turned the courtyard into a hemisphere of salt, slammed the rain down hard and subdued winter into a metallic blackness. These forces called upon him whenever he wished to unleash them on the occupants of the house, chiefly Bonny, Ray and Zella. In short, he developed the genius to turn everyone's pain into his epic pomp.

It started in the summer of 1985 when he began to ascend on the house with the sun in a slow explosion of breathlessly blinding heat. The chief ingredient of his burden was sweat with which he charged the temperature of his unpredictability. What he was doing was so intense that even the fridge failed to form ice. Ray in his voiceless world and Zella in her wordless one were always waking up on the edge of nightmares, always rendezvousing with dangerous sleep.

Only God sees time lines and it seems He takes time to turn things around but actually He moves way faster than the fastest wheels of wind. Beyond the screen of shadows, His light glowed faintly far. In order to reach it, Ray elevated to faith for the time being from his taboo paths and asked Him to take him out of there.

God has eagle hands. He lifted him and put him in a place that was a miniature civilisation in its own right, a place so mythological that even God's autograph appeared to be thin there. But then He had already taught him that every beginning is underpinned by an end. He also discovered that the world is more fantastic ahead than the one before.

Once Bonny had been a man of poetic persuasion. Once he could catch the sky by its Achilles heel, that is the horizon and train it to be giddy with his poetry and songs from dawn to dusk but that was in the Province of Ignorance. Now as the last surrogate winter gave birth to a spring, his mind became full of holes. He stood and swayed like a pendulous giddy dinosaur as the men from *Nurmanzil* arrived to carry Yogesh away to the psychiatric institution. It was like putting a cyclone through the eye of a darning needle.

3

To the sagging house of transmogrification came the Vice Principal, Dalton D'Costa, like a patron saint of morning with the engravings of heaven on his face and starless eyes. Below that surface were several other surfaces.

'You need to rest.'

Rest in peace he meant with bell chimes in his voice.

'I can adapt.'

Bonny felt a new intensity for a few seconds that magnified the symptoms of his Parkinsonism.

'It is not about survival.'

Dalton D'Costa taught English but he never gave up squeezing into others' territory like the bugs he juiced.

'And as I can see from your condition, I feel, you are struggling to survive.' But it was Bonny who harvested the rewards of poetry in three languages English, Hindi and Urdu.

'Abhi is chiraag me tel baaki hai aur abhi thodi raat bhi baaki hai…'

Dalton D'Costa put on a heartlessly smooth administrative surface and cut off the couplet midway with a cutting edge rock solid voice.

'Mr. Deut, all I am saying is you need to be fit when it is obvious that you are not.'

And at that point Bonny shook even more unfavourably and shed secret black tears for his son who had to be admitted to *Nurmanzil* a second time.

'See you.'

Dalton D'Costa's polished summary speech was now clearly on top of his gentle willing tone of help.

4

The new Principal, TW Schlepps, had the genetics of a passing ghost.

'You have to resign.'

He had a kind of leaping shape with poison spots for eyes.

'You have time till the end of May.'

A little bit of heaven crumbled whenever he spoke. Exotic sins were embarrassed when he moved. Dalton D'Costa, the hunter of eyeless bugs, had the last word in his urbanite accent.

'Please vacate the house.'

Bonny felt like a fetus of estranged love trapped in heaps of thick melancholy mucous. At home he picked up the Word and spent the day trying to reach a compromise with the termites which had made so many holes in his life. At night, in his dreams, darkness blinked like the black board in his lab on which lightning etched, like a blind piece of chalk, the ending of his life's saga and he clung with fantastic hands to the edge of reality and escaped the drift of a falling veil.

He resigned and vacated the house. Victoria and Ray arrived to help in the task. The truck was loaded. The three of them squeezed into the back with Zella under the furniture and plunged into the night. It would have been a normal event to reach their home in the Province of Ignorance by the morning but Bonny did not have the strength to keep pace with the journey. Belief is also a kind of motion. Bonny was no longer reconciled to the belief that he would be able to make it.

Animals who have grown up as pets are more aware of the secret knowledge of human existence. Zella whined and came out suddenly from below the tangle of household things and embraced him tightly as Bonny passed out of his body into the achromatic headlights of the oncoming traffic. Ray tried to resuscitate him and Victoria rubbed his hands and face but he was beyond their control. Zella slipped back and down into the depths as the theory of meaning gradually became inconsistent with the rest of the road. It was 2 am.

5

The bleached white graves behind Teacher's Row seemed to have been hewn out of the bleached white houses of the Teacher's Row. Winged night sat like a solitary sculpture over each, undeterred by the framework of weed-embracing crosses. The hours crawled like prey towards its predator until it was two am in the Province of Ignorance.

Strangely, death, an offspring of sleep, never rests and on that night it played its unchanging refrain over diffused dreams of sweet fancy's mystery colours. They faded and the aggravating ones piled up on the eyelids and Aru began to experience a headlong drop into one of them. Her nightmare escorted the friendless solitary truck on the road from the City of Constantia.

Its headlamps flickered like glimpses of hell's eye-lamps. While outside the house, opposite the pipal tree, a quaking wave of sheathed faces and forms, led by an all-consuming effulgence, alighted. The intensity sweated a velvety breeze through the trees. A twig or two snapped. A sigh enunciated her name.

By the time she became fully aware of it, night had again become annoyingly desolate and darkness strained stiffly like the curiously quiet hounds in the back and front courtyards. She picked her way bare feet through the disquieting but familiar torments of the house and came out into the courtyard. A pair of vigilant muzzles attended to her, their eyes shining like insular stars as she unlocked the main door and stepped into the still aura of the other worldly terrain and stood in the street light under the pipal.

A hand had knocked and a voice had called but where were the face and the form to match them?

The kiss of death sank its lips into her cheek and an age lapsed before the swamp of understanding began to swallow her up. She closed the door on the choking heap of the rustic country and returned to the safety of the bed. A relieving calm fell back on her and she ignored the double edged night. Fear had quailed before her courage. Finally, consciousness vanished like an infant's innocence and gradually, the usual crusty clamours of the night resumed with a bark and a hoot and a baying and a yowl.

6

'Even if you call me at 2 o' clock in the night, I'll be there.' Raman Prakash's words assumed the countenance of destiny on that middle of nowhere road which ate its way very slowly into the bigoted morning. It is a virtue not to align tears with a shrill wailing in order to be understood but a sob of grief is as comprehensible as the iambic odes of grinding Gahanna.

Victoria and Ray waded through the desideratum of sorrow in quiet decency. The comfort of each other's closeness and the cure of being left alone to grieve became a memory of the shared journey. They did, however, waver between furious desperation to seek help somewhere, somehow on the way and the reserved passivity to stop at the only hospital they knew. They chose the latter.

The Mission Hospital hummed exotically but emptily at the edge of the Province of Ignorance. It was more crammed with memories than doctors, nurses and patients.

The combined effect of rigor mortis and Parkinsonism had rendered Bonny's fingers into fixed tormented gnarls over his chest and they had to be strapped to his torso after the doctor declared his death in a flat, low voice. With assistance from a kind soul, the truck was guided, in the meanwhile, to the house opposite the pipal tree. Aru opened the door in a wholehearted welcome.

'Where are my mother, father and brother?'

She sought cheerful news from the kind soul.

'They are coming.'

The kind soul's soothing tone was more haunting. And then Aru saw the crawling casualty, consuming the landscape. The air around it lost its crispiness and the horizon hung haggardly. It was like a tortured wound, torn from a crucifixion, held high, atop a little procession, her mother and brother on either side of the wrapped up body. In the stew of their sorrow, Victoria and Ray's faces floated in the muddled summer morning, bearing undisguisedly and blatantly, an expression of the journey of another kind.

Aru immediately collapsed in a swoon.

7

The house opposite the pipal tree turned into an empty pit of disorder into which Peeping Toms peeped. Others hastened in and out of the house with obvious surprise and shock, wincing at the right places in its story. A few others, more passionate, came and stood, trying not to disturb those who were already tormenting themselves, boiling like soda on white sheets on the floor. It is better to be crucified than to sit through a crucifixion.

With high noon, water from the inexhaustible ice slabs below the string cot rose into a high tide. The course of conversation cut loose from loud tributes to smothered judgments. Yet the end could not be revised despite all the nagging pity or unkind words for disowned Adam, severed from the world of the living.

'We were right.'

Time's constantly losing momentum does not affect everything. The dead-end doll faces of melancholy remain the same.

'We knew it from the beginning.'

Their industry of denunciation remains the same.

'It was a mistake to leave this place.'

Founders of conflict, they turn into temporary monks, a waiting priesthood, when the belly of the land heaves, opens up its mouth and swallows one of them and when the earth becomes normal again, that is, when in a toned down odium of biological evolution, the unfortunate derivative of Eve has turned into worms, they too slip back into their physical arrangements of order and disorder.

'It is a failed house.'

With pronouncements like those, they derived conversation from each alphabet of their memory until they had a full text of Bonny Deut's short life on their tongues.

'Let this be an example.'

8

In the day's growing heat, Death's dough turned waxen. A blurred crow quivered desolately above. Inside, praise and criticism dwindled into an effervescence. Outside, the coffin makers lumbered heavily under Mr. J. Pal but at the back, the grave diggers' shovels wore down deeper and deeper into the dark and dry pit.

The vibrations of the new world reached Zella, curled up under a familiar piece of furniture, watching nonexistence and existence at play from the end of her tail. Dogs' opinions are counted zero because they are unable to express conservative shock, unlike dishonest mammals, their masters. Absence of tragedy in a dog's life is as false as freedom of comedy in human life. Survival was an indefinite thing until she could find a lawful buffer between her and several savage beasts somewhere in the house, whose presence she was beginning to become aware of.

As the day plummeted towards sunset, an impervious crowd made the otherwise wide door narrow, even blocking it at times. The padre with his widespread polished face and girth descended on everyone with his articles of faith and the book of burial. He represented a trace of spirituality right at the end when he read, '.......earth to earth, ashes to ashes, dust to dust......' but up to that point he went through the process with the administrative preoccupation of quickly putting the dead away with a mad thought crossing his head even in those moments of trying at least once to resurrect the dead.

But it was only a thought and he dismissed it quickly with another thought: *I am not Jesus. Turning death into life is a thing of faith which I don't have.*

Death brings famine. Hunger becomes even more assertive in a time of sorrow. It separates the earnest mourner from the deliberate ones. Behind Ray's guise of pain, an aching lingered, an emptiness that grew with the gravedigger's gash in the ground at the back. The greedy ground swallowed the digger for the time being but Ray looked for some food in the house. Aru's vacant expression said that he could munch on the void for all she cared. The untouched tiffins his mother had prepared for the journey were in the fridge but he dared not disturb them.

9

An ashen whiteness covered Bonny's face like makeup and when blood oozed like a ghost's silhouette from one of the nostrils, cotton swabs were pushed into them. For the other unseen perforations, clouds of perfume misted the air from time to time, until the air itself turned sickly sweet.

The aim of death is the same as that of life: To undertake the next journey. The dials clocked up to 5 o'clock and Bonny's lips tightened like the narrow gauge track along Teacher's Row. A train passed by like a premonition. Impending kisses reached his forehead and cheeks amidst a farewell buzz. Friendly hands gently slid the coffin lid over him and the nails dug into its edges, sealing belief in life in overwhelming blackness of the satin outside and a commitment to the abysmal colours of bottomlessness inside and this climate of the final end turned everything into the apparatus of death: candles and flowers and perfumes. It was a well planned departure. Bonny had written about it in his poems.

Meri kashti ki nakamyabi ko dekho
Kinare aa ke doobi ja rahi hai...

Victoria got up. Tears could never define her. The race she was built out of did not know fatigue, sorrow or defeat. She surprised even light with the clarity of her eyes and with her rose to their feet the founders of memory whose buffer tongues created long unreal shapes out of brief real lives. The padre led the mourning wanderers like a navigator, reading from his little book of rites. People drifted under the coffin box by turns with death's spontaneity. The march to the grave was quick and soon the active crowd surrounded the inert box now resting on a plank over the rectangular hole. Among them were those who are always uninvited, excluded from all life and death's events but turn up anyway perhaps because they themselves never knew a birth and they would never have a funeral.

The apathetic gravediggers adjusted the stiff ropes to lower the box. Lifeless, dispirited clods rolled down onto the wood. The padre, that supposed promoter of eternal life, picked up a few brittle pieces of earth and on his cue so did everyone else and rained them down in a slow shower of vague purport. The thrust of dust smothered the padre's last prayer in a thin film until finally billowing flowers, candles and incense sticks lit up their faces. Twilight stood on tiptoe behind them all. The zenith surged and ripped itself in a flash as an age came to an end.

10

'Such a thing has happened to us! What a haadsaa!!' Aru was still dizzy though she did not need diversion to get back to her usual state of idleness. The potpourri of conversation was only a supplement to long spells of silence. Victoria showed them the journey-food-and-water. It had turned tangibly black like emotional garbage. There was a pause when the sensitive tan of the twilight passed into the fair hands of a neighbor holding a cool glass of orange squash to Ray's mouth. He was so enamoured by her that he could not take his eyes off her heels too. The moisture of that juice lingered for a long time on his lips and agile and eager shadows began to persevere against its pointlessness.

Zella emerged from some such shadows and was immediately seized by the evening clamor of sparrows, parrots, crows, chickens, mice and the backyard dogs but found her balance and continued on her exploration of the rooms and the front courtyard. The anesthetic dinner came from a sympathetic neighbour. It blunted elevation of any kind and the rest of the evening dwindled from laconic to a silent passing. Finally the lights were off and the doors sealed and the night began to read each eye's chronicles of the day. The inconvenience of an unfamiliar bed did not handicap sleep.

Only the ill-advised close their eyes to deep sleep on such a night because even the most fortified town of snores cannot stonewall the whole entourage of unguarded dreams. They rally and spur their unsaddled horses, encompassing the individual with their occult wraiths. They grew upon Ray in this fashion like inverted commas until he stirred and heard himself agree with their speech with a loud enough 'haaan', that is, a 'yes'. Victoria, in the little adjacent room, heard and called his name out.

'Ray?'

He opened his eyes.

'Who are you talking to?'

The night overloaded the empty bedroom with cramping chaos but he answered her through sleep-clenched lips.

'No one, Ma!'

After that, an interval: A stage course of space. A time of whiles. A termed stretch of an odour.

'Can you smell it, Ray?' Aru asked from her bed in the drawing room.

It followed the spell of its increase until the whole house was full of it.

'Aru and Ray!'

Victoria aviated urgently.

'Pray.'

Like an angel of hovering protection over them from her tiny room.

11

The morning was dewy on the hot sticky bodies of sleepless sweat but very soon the sun began to rage down fire and to bake the day on each brick. Victoria went about her work with a soft, gloss-incrusted glance. She did not wait for alleviation from suffering. Any further weakening of the will crippled the signal fulfilment of function and duty. Even with her husband's untimely and bitter demise, she did not throw away immunity to a sense of loss. Powerfully spirited and only a little earthly minded, she took hold of each day's winning. One hundred percent work-wrangled, nothing could chip away her peace of mind.

The door opened and a little scowling angel poked his head in, followed by his older sibling with her plunging lip line and drooping eyes, followed by their mother's combination of the two expressions and at the end, by a man of populous uncertainties well covered by his French cut. Aru and Ray's hearts swelled up with joy at the sight of their Didi even in the atmosphere of inconvenient grief but into which Charu quietly allowed herself to dissolve. Sami, however, got into a steam and a storm. He was the kind of bug that Dalton D'Costa would have loved to catch and crush in his pocket. But, except Charu, he was nobody else's humble crush.

12

The concert of compromise was ready to star Yogesh once again. By the time he was brought home, they had already scrubbed the last sign of grief from the floors. Now, all he had to do was to watch himself battle ciphers. But he was impeded by confusion. By doubts.

No one wanted to treat him like a leftover, but keeping a respectful distance between themselves and him, they kept bursting their bubbles of love and concern all around him but the diffused memories of Bonny in the City of Constantia could not reconcile him to the house in the Province of Ignorance.

'Where's Daddy?'

The question was sudden but they answered it with conservative labor, carefully embroidering the rough edges of Bonny's death. He visited the grave in the hot afternoon with Ray. Dust lathered the trail behind them and uprooted weeds twitched like whales of guilt, whacking themselves to death. It was all too ridiculous. The distances did not release him too, to start afresh on a clean slate. He did not know if he was at the bottom of a beginning or the top of an end.

A hushed gap fell between him and them in which he tried to sleep off the effects of the whole thing and in which a dream hatched every now and then and everyone else also pretended to effect a sleep because when they were awake he could see that they were all thinking how to hurriedly run the course of things. They watched him from across canyons of misery. There was no new ground to break. No foundation to strengthen. Nothing to bring to pass. Like pious flies, they only loaded their throats with lumps of emotional prayers and a swollen gathering of tears over terminologies of depression.

He was caught by surprise when they expressed their compulsion to do something for him.

'He must be kept busy.'

'Ray you take him to Delhi.'

'Ma, get him a job in a school here.'

'Aru talk to your principal, Mrs. Raman Prakash.'

Ultimately, Charu was seized by an idea.

'There is no one to play the church piano in our College.'

'And he can also teach music to the students.' Sami added, never expecting a crown of compensation for his life-saving suggestion and at which blithe antics of grin gas accompanied deep sighs of relief.

That night, fine spun sleep, like twilight froth made a beginning and also an end. Yogesh lacked any excitement for it to peak. Next day, was Sunday and annihilation was the main feature of the sermon. The hymns exerted entreaty against divine purge.

13

God's design cannot be destroyed and eternity is never unclear about any address across the face of the Earth. But with what despair, the weather's slow shuffle corresponded between dizzy airlessness and echoing winds on judgment call, that soon enough, the whispering muses of the Monsoon began to sing from memory, old songs of thunder and lightning!! The two angel-faced children with brooding brows alternated between their parents, uncles and aunt's appalling sense of fate and the calm endurance of their grandmother, Victoria. To them Yogesh was a simulated apparition, the mirror feature of a cracked dice.

'What has happened to Yogesh Mamu?' Sana, the elder one asked in her sweet sap-like voice.

Charu's smile shot out like a parallel rainbow. The younger sibling, Simeon, who had noticed Bonny's old arm chair, was curious too. An umbilical red mark on his face swelled with his question.

'Is it grandfather's?'

Hallucinations of Babel!!

'How does he know that?'

'Did he ever see papa sit in it?'

'Never!!'

Unanalyzed amazement lingered for a long time at what the little boy had asked but nobody answered his question. The umbilical red mark on his face shrank back without further incident. It was like a captive shadow, a lingering suspension of coveted virtues, one of them being, withholding speech for long periods of time. That's what he did. He became the custodian of a choking silence and never asked anything about that chair again even though he and his sister's lives revolved around it for almost two years in that house as they were going to stay with their grandmother and aunt.

Little children bring about a mediation between those who want to get on with the bustling business of daily life and the custodians of apparitions. Their innocent awkwardness is a catalyst of change in the lives of those who forget that awkwardness is not a handicap. Yogesh was not a little child and his awkwardness bound him up and no one around him was qualified to deal with it. At best it could be disguised. Trying to stifle the whole essence of a man like Yogesh!! Despair the man who would want to do that alone: Sami. Charu was going to be in Delhi in pursuit of a higher degree while her children would stay in the Province of Ignorance.

'But first I will go with you both.' Charu said soothingly to him.

'Okay, if you want to come, though you can leave with Ray. I can handle everything,' Sami said, oblivious to the dangers that emanated from his confidence about handling Yogesh. He had no knowledge that the latter was not a mere physical entity. Victoria reflected over Sami's assurance.

'Don't neglect his medicines.'

Sami moved his supple lips reassuringly.

'You don't worry.'

And so Victoria bustled about preparing for their journey. Soon enough big bags and suitcases full of her love and care stood at the threshold. They stepped out of the house. Charu and Sami and Yogesh. Their faces polished like the mirror moon, not yet reflecting the far end of this venture but it came close in haunting whirls as they began to exchange kisses. The rickshaws arrived and with all the luggage and the passengers, they began to look like two intractable mules, irreconcilable to their burdens. Victoria and Ray looked at their backs for long. Sami and then Charu looked back once but Yogesh did not.

Those on time's journey never turn and look back. Funny thing about time's journey: it may be short or long but one of its ends keeps disappearing from view.

The stationary train looked like an assortment of people, compartments, engine and luggage. A patchwork of rectangular lights and oblong pieces of darkness but when it began to move, it blended into a yawning stew of continuous, swirling night in which gaps of light changed from the codes of dusk to dawn. Next evening, Ray, the inventor of mercurial retrogression, left for Delhi.

14

Prudence simmered in the foreground and noisily conjuring, expressionless creatures converged in the background, zeroing in on the irreversible truth that Yogesh was beyond redemption. In the garish dimness of the railway compartment, Charu instructed her husband.

'Sami, take good care of my brother.'

Sami grunted like the predestined train going full-mouthed towards its aim. Soon deep sleep began to combust its fuel and scorching dreams of the night parched the throats but no one woke up to quench the drought. Blind miles swallowed up the bright-eyed train. Barren wraiths of land and trees and houses and huts spumed past the dark windows. The nimble train constantly hammered away at the track rivets, producing now and then euphoric sparks.

The dismissive lights woke up Yogesh and he found himself surrounded by the journey's critical reality. His mind retreated into a safe state of idleness that restrained him from looking forward to the end of the journey. Charu stirred but he did not fall into any pretense to close his eyes or to look away.

Camouflage was a trick of temptation. He was not attracted to it. Deft spirits like Ray used it as cover. And yet, nobody could steer deception the way they wanted. For shallow and profound purposes. He pulled the sheet like a mantle. Revelation was about swallowing masks. He watched Sami snore. For some, sleep was a hold and hinder command unlike Charu who was a sagacious sage who read life as a mock yarn with vacant trivial wishes and vague cradle to grave sites.

Like sharp unerring posterns, the Lal Kothi gates always remained open. Charu and Sami's residence was in the corner on the first floor of the huge red brick building. Behind it, the edge of the city screamed day and night and lives smelted in its long u-shaped, common verandas on hot Sunday afternoons.

'Don't worry about anything. I will visit you from time to time. Write to me if you have any problem.'

Charu's genuine and gentle concern offset Sami's direct deftness. With those words she delivered Yogesh into Sami's care and left. Sami, that is, Samson Shaun, Yogesh's host, was a careful concentrate of circumspect intention. He was a shrewd deliverer of services. Breakfast, lunch and dinner on time. Clothes washed, dried, picked up and pressed every day. Beds made and the house neatened up day and night. It was all done with honest motivation without sly wariness ever creeping up on him. His craft synergy was brimful but not with even the slightest hint of cold coveting. He was only like the moon at night trying to model itself after the sun on the other side. He watched Yogesh with a circumspect desire to only learn.

Yogesh's dispirited leaven did not rise until on the first Sunday. He was landed in the chapel by Sami and a choir of nurses, starched in youthfulness, zoomed in on him immediately. After the service, they practiced with him at the piano and the funk impulse of their virgin hearts beat into the notes of the hymns. Even the truly gifted have to deal with a raspy muse but he was encouraged by Sami to sharpen it for his new fans' sake.

'They love you.'

Sami strove like a secret highlight under Yogesh's spotlight. It was a swell sight to watch the young pianist trying to deal with so much praise angling into flattery. But compliments alone do not feed a life like that of Yogesh. The time for that was long gone and with it his need to be creative and inventive for the sake of women.

The formula was thickening.

15

The mornings' stirring quietness yielded to a simmering, stifling drift. It became a deliberate torture to seek comfort in the empty house during the weekdays after Sami left for work. The breakfast was laid on the dining table and the medicines with the instructions on a slip beside it. By the time he got up and came to the table, the tea had thinned into a travesty and the omelet shrunk into a green greyness. He picked up the medicines and wandered through the house, looking at each and every object that made the house a deliberate parody of home and family. It propelled him to the bathroom.

A faceless essence stared back at him from the mirror and hours of self-reflection overflowed like wasted water. He stood, poring over the imprecise medicines, slowly dissolving and draining in the sink. The affliction of the hours drove him to the chapel where he gave an account of his mental state on the piano keyboard and after hours of thoroughly dissecting and diagnosing himself with hymnal music, he achieved a relative, tentative but contemplative peace. Every day it sustained him for hours. Without food, without medicines.

At the end, however, hunger found its target. It always does and then it becomes a source of agitation as food is used both as a tool and a gauge of control. The hand with the ladle is the sum total of all control. With every morsel he took, Yogesh thought Sami's stranglehold on him was growing but which was only the latter's haunting sense of duty, who, as soon as he returned in the evening, immediately set about work in the kitchen, the bathroom and the rest of the house, thinking of delegating some of it to Yogesh. It began with the TV which is anyway a poor prop to sustain any relationship. When Yogesh watched it, Sami dusted it. Then one day, he suggested a role reversal.

'Would you like to do the dusting?'

But Yogesh was on a tight schedule. Sami, absolutely unaware, was trying to stretch it.

'Would you put out the washing?' And 'Please pick up the washing.'

It was a mistake to send him to the roof. Yogesh dealt with the chronicles of clothes on the clothesline but he also reviewed the bright sun and was filled with a kindling turmoil and flaming tumult to sweat-revel on the hot bricks.

16

He was on the edge of Genesis. In the beginning...... God created light and Yogesh was attracted to it. The idea that he could spend more time on the roof gradually fastened itself around his head and the obligation to play the present, according to Sami's rules, was gradually spent. He subdued his needs by treating eating as a handicap. The TV into an odd idle object. And conversation a full-mouthed act of exhaustion. He only worked at further metamorphosis. Desolation began to propose. Distress in another costume came and stood, waiting.

Sami addressed him abruptly and businesslike.

'How was your day?'

The echo killed all attempts at conversation.

'How was your day?'

They continued to go to the chapel on weekends. A little abbreviated by him but obliged by the giggling girls, he accepted his lesser position as Yogesh's manager.

'He is so soft spoken.'

They crooned and hung about Yogesh, haranguing him to teach them to play music.

'He is so sweet.'

He obliged but none of them learnt anything. Finally the brothers-in-law returned home to resume contemplating the fizz of strangeness.

Perfection has something to do with stature. Its capacity is greater in little people. That was Charu. It made her unyielding to the things Sami, also a perfectionist, was prey to. It made her, his legendary piper. Her letters quickened him with wisdom. Her visits delighted him with only a quantum of her fury.

The rumble of caution in her correspondence grew.

You don't need a genius of physical might, which you are, to deal with Yogesh.

The line and length of the letters conveyed her understanding of the whole thing.

God is the only remedy.

The opacity of the relationship between the brothers-in-law.

He is the only reward.

She detected his helplessness from the twisted intestines of his handwriting in his letters.

Pray to Him.

17

She landed one weekend when he was praying. Yogesh was asleep. One look at him in profile and she knew. When it came to expressing anger, she was an orthodox.

'I don't think he is taking his medicines.'

Sami thought of some advertising disclaimers.

'I myself give him the night doze.'

But did not utter them.

'What about the afternoon?'

He moved the huge heaps of his hands in a saga of their own.

'I am not here in the afternoon but I keep it on the dining table and it is not there when I return.'

Charu gave him an unsparingly austere stare.

'I am sure he is taking the afternoon doze too. I asked him and he said that he takes them regularly.'

He shoved more bricks into the heat of her eyes.

'Do you give him my letters to read?'

He had stacked them up like a thick journal on the rack.

'I don't stop him from reading them.'

She thumbed through them, dropping one or two.

'Why don't you ask him to write me a line or two?'

He dashed down like pure lightning and picked them up.

'I don't stop him from writing to you.'

And handed them to her with thoughtless surrender.

'Does he go to the chapel as and when he feels?'

He avoided looking at her.

'Everyday.'

She could cut him up into pieces with her gaze.

'Does he teach the choir?'

Erudition softened them up a bit.

'He enjoys that.'

She adjusted her glasses on her nose. Scholars are bad at accepting confessions.

'And so do *you!*'

She tried to imagine him sitting with his guitar, basking in the glow of the handsome, young singer and musician, ignoring the flirtatious girls.

18

Fury grows fat on babble. Neither is solitude alleviating. Yogesh's routine of restlessness was growing like a yawn. Sami nagged Charu for a solution.

Take him to mother during the holidays, she instructed, and bring the children with you.

'I am taking you to your mother during the holidays.' Sami's announcement suddenly proposed to Yogesh, access to an illuminated exit.

'I can go myself.' Yogesh made an arcane suggestion.

'But I have to bring Sana and Simeon with me. Their mother will be visiting during the holidays and they would want to meet her.'

Yogesh's agreement passed in reluctant silence. If he had a wish, it met with a plausible, primitive end. But it was a forerunner of some oblique thing that he would bring into effect sooner or later. The game of liberation could be played in a roundabout way. It was just a matter of time. For now, he had to wage peace so that even the most discerning person, Charu, would fail to notice it.

Dusk was reciting the last lesson of the day and night was getting ready to do its divisions when they reached Victoria's house. Aru had just been scolding both the children for a squabble over homework. She opened the door with the look of a class monitor but lost it when she saw who it was outside. With a muffled cry of surprise, she gave in to Sami's snug embrace and kisses. Yogesh still looked like a tongue-tied and hesitant cherub, slightly blurred by the moonlight and showed no inclination to kiss or to be kissed. She led them into the house. The two children on perceiving both men remained riveted like a pair of divine deities.

'He is your Mamu! Greet and kiss him!!'

They did so.

'And he is your father! Greet and kiss him!'

But they found it quite pointless to do that and stood evenly with their infant like mutinous smiles. Sami kissed Victoria gingerly and followed her about the house with a facile chat about all the things he was doing for Yogesh. Victoria irradiated her motherly love and care around her son during the vacation. Her succor did not yet kindle in him a desire to talk.

19

The whispering waves of autumn took away the holidays and brought Sami back with the children. They looked the same. Emotionally split from everyone and glossily bored with themselves. Aru squeezed them in an embrace but they deferred responding to her love as warmly as she would have wanted them to. In the meanwhile, Victoria set up her stall of blessings and stretched a glance at Sami who knew she was preparing to address him.

'Sami, is my son happy there?'

'Oh yes.'

His answers lit a fuse in Yogesh's mind.

'Does he take his medicines regularly?'

'I make sure he does.'

His answer pleased her greatly and she loaded him with gifts.

'Beta, do you listen to Sami and do whatever he says?'

Obedience is an act of reciprocation that springs from connections but Yogesh's mind was a terminating void. Turning. Shifting. Rotating. Sami was a connection that had never formed.

'He listens to me.' Sami answered on his behalf.

A meditative repulsion welled up within Yogesh. He would have to cast the net of disorder on this creature. The direction of Yogesh's ire was determined but he put on an agreeable countenance for the journey back. The distance was irrelevant. Time was irrelevant. He had become an entity that did not want love. He had no will. No wish. No preferences. There was no prize for him in this world. And so, they withdrew from Victoria's home like extracts from a literary passage into the oblivion of wordlessness.

Ample words and empty talk are alluring to some. While to others, the ambit of silence. Speech springs a surprise in such a scenario. Yogesh's silence was expanding, affecting volumes of confidence of his host. If it was a strategy, Sami was confused.

'What is it?' He asked.

Yogesh whispered down a sharp response.

Not yet. Not yet.

'What do you want? Have I done something wrong?'

Sami made it sound like a moral matter but he did not know that Yogesh had reached a moment of complete cease. No connection whatsoever could be reached, no matter what he tried. Without the occurrence of human sounds, the house was turning into an ambiguous zone of brooding atmosphere. Sami's position as host became indefensible when Yogesh stopped eating with him.

Am I going to permit this? Sami asked himself.

Like a colossal fly, the advancing dark dusk was picking up a full flutter on his household. The proof came, when, one day, Sami returned in the afternoon and did not find him in the house. The breakfast and the tablets lay untouched on the table. He was not in the chapel.

Has he gone to the market? But he has no money!

Sami finally found him on the roof, seminude in the dabbling, moist, sweaty sunlight.

'What are you doing here?'

Silence dripped in perspiration.

'Do you want to go back?'

He was held back by the bounds of forfeiture.

'Are you unhappy here?'

His voice almost failed.

'Have I made you upset?'

The smooth circle of the sun completely encompassed Yogesh and Sami disappeared in the furtherance of his own languishing.

20

Sami did not yet feel like a blind bird before a cat. There would be time for that yet. He called up Charu.

'Come immediately and talk to your brother.'

She, who interpreted infinity, advised caution.

'I'll come shortly.'

Sami ached with dishonor.

'Everyone is talking.'

Even as the volatile sun-figure sharpened his sweat upstairs.

'Our house has become the talk of the town.'

The thin binding of the bloodless tie made Sami feel very weak.

'I am so helpless. He is *your* brother. Please come immediately.'

Charu passed observance of discretion as an executive order.

'Act wisely!'

Strangely, however, wisdom is synoptic.

'I will come as soon as I am free.'

It is just not there in the details.

'Okay.'

But everything connected to Yogesh was like a tight constraint.

'I will try.'

There were no details.

Sami's own blood began to beat narrowly. Time's tiny capillaries were cramping it from reaching his brain. He came out. Lal Kothi appeared like a jumbled up nest. He went up and watched Yogesh from a distance. A breathless breeze puzzled over the latter's smooth face. A disconnected tree, stretching over the far end of the terrace, stammered inarticulate things into the breeze. A league of demons ground a grin into the bare bricks.

Where is the Lord of creation?

A frown sorted itself out of the tangle of Sami's brow. He came down and sat in a chair, his silence indistinguishable from the stillness of the house, listening to the muffled footsteps of the luminous afternoon wandering around on the uneven bricks overhead. He had never felt so lost. So barren and obsolete. He wondered about his useless and stagnant life.

What makes Yogesh and his ilk so different? Are they human? Why do they at all integrate themselves into human affairs? Would he, Sami, ever be able to smear an impression on the grand scheme of things so that he too would never be ignored, forgotten and disregarded? For a spiritual rise and shine, he would have to tread the dangerous, wild and weary path that sometimes vanishes from sight. But the corrupt settling of hell in the deep details of life removes any inclination to be morally upright. In ways, unconforming to the world. Irreconcilable to the end of ones days. In speech, jarring.

And in stature, unsuitable like a whale in a gold fish bowl.

21

The sun disentangled itself from the squeeze of sweat and began to inch away from the red brick house, allowing commodious darkness to retouch everything. Sami had dinner and watched the TV for some time. Its sounds slammed about in his head for some time until he was satisfied by the lack of reason. Waiting was pointless.

'I can't wait anymore!'

He went to the door and came out into the long, dim and empty corridor. Each detail of the night narrated the design of muddle. He stood confused for a few seconds, then bolted the net door and switched off the lights. The faintly unlit house seemed secure against the uncertainties of the night but he would wrest his portion of sleep from it and let the darkness rage in pitiless dreams outside.

He was right. Dreams, like sketchy paintings, recited their images of ruin, which would have imparted great satisfaction to the ghosts of the great painters. Concentrated night suspended the wavering moon for the rest of the hours and a taming chill oscillated over the prone figure on the roof. Then darkness itself was substituted. There was a shift. A gradual unwinding.

A cast off skin fell away. An off-key night bird creaked like wood close by as a many sided irregularity separated from the roof's floor and slid down the steps and scratched through a crack in the wire mesh of the door into the house like an itch and slipped into the bed in the adjacent room. By first light, it had absorbed its deep cunning into a human resemblance. Morning released its light into the house and Sami woke up. He went into the next room and could not believe his eyes.

'How in the world…!'

It would be as an anecdote that Sami would relate many months later to the family when they would meet again but that morning it filled him with a disquiet. With what ease a human can become incompatible with earthly things was beginning to confound and convince him. He examined the screen door. There was a tiny crack in one corner for perhaps only a small cat to crawl through. An intense mother of curiosity hung behind Sami's dull mask, waiting for Yogesh to get up which he did ultimately but not as a consequence of Sami's impatience.

'How did you get inside the house?'

Yogesh was immune to such inquisitiveness. He bound a smile down with redefined silence, a moderate gaze and an unhemmed lungi. With these he contained Sami whose handicap at understanding what he was dealing with grew while he gave his *tapasya* a staple thrust by leaving the terrace and stretching out in the ground in full view of the residents. Sami sounded the alert promptly.

'This is as low as it can get.'

He was in the grip of a toilsome seizure.

'Why can't you talk to him?'

An unseasoned contempt welled up within Charu.

'Did you say or do anything to provoke it?'

The receiver crackled with bad weather.

'I don't know!'

She sensed his self-condemnation.

'Tell him to stop it immediately! I am coming.'

His veins stood out on his forehead in turbulent tide but he felt empowered and went down. Yogesh opened one eye under the shelter of the all seeing eye in the sky. Sami tried to blot the latter with his tall frame and the silence of the onlookers with an unrehearsed holler.

'Please stop all this and come inside!!'

The utterance disturbed the solemnity of the event.

'Your Didi is coming!'

Until she did, future waited like a sharp pinpoint to pierce the present. The eye, however, concluded the conversation by closing.

22

Next day, Charu came tumbling and booming into the house, a light travelling bag in one hand and went straight to Yogesh. He was accommodated under the sun like a yogi of great esteem. A vacuum began to blow hotly around him.

'Stop doing all this tamasha immediately!'

It caught up the Lal Kothi residents in its swirling whirlwind.

'Don't you care for anybody's position?'

The nucleus of all the curiosity, soaked up the surrounding energy like a sponge.

'What will you achieve by this?'

His muse sang while his elder sibling screamed.

'Get up and go inside the house right now!'

Finally his voice emerged from the stew of abstinence.

'Give me money so I can go away.'

She shook a finger at Sami who had turned into some sort of a mild substratum.

'No! Sami will accompany you back.'

Yogesh replied with a cynical emptiness.

'Who is he?'

She turned away and climbed up the stairs to her house in consummate helplessness.

'What a shame!'

Sami followed and there was an outbreak of tongue lashing inside but his faithful adherence to his wife's loving outbursts sustained him through the rest of the day.

'Lock him up inside the house when you go for work.'

The end is also an opening. Sami saw it briefly.

'What will he do?'

Consciousness has a past.

'Maybe nothing.'

But for each individual, it has no precedent. The future cannot be predicted. Only God knows everything. Charu and Sami felt very strongly the 'not knowing' moment but did not buckle before its power.

'Inform me if anything happens.'

And she left, releasing him into the extremely gnarled future. That night, sleep's circumspect invasion gave Sami some relief and he got up earlier than usual to turn the house into a clanging, infringing prison.

23

Destiny is a winged creature. Ready and swift to strike. It takes off from the pages of some endless, unread, meaningless poem. How could Sami have recourse to it? Revelation ignored him the whole day but it fed the dissembling heat of the closed rooms as the sun rose higher and higher, over and around the house in Lal Kothi.

On alert scrutiny, a shadow under the doors and behind the windows, tracked the ancient convoy of stars along their paths, splitting through the mist of human unease, marveling at the suppression of distinct evidence that everything is predetermined. It was attended by the softened refrain of a rattle of the locked door, advertising a disturbance to the neighbours from time to time. Finally, the impetuous haste of heat worked towards tolerance and an ease of peace by sunset.

The ministers of the mind never foster a prayer. Sami began to pray when it was time for him to head home.

'The Lord is my shepherd….'

Nameless terrors went up the steps with him.

'Deliver us from evil…..'

He felt he needed an escort of angels as he tended to the last part of the Lord's Prayer.

'For thine is the Kingdom, the Power and the Glory…. forever and ever.'

The assistants of hurry gradually fell behind and he became so slow that for a long time he stood before the door alone, fumbling for the key. The address was right. The angle was wrong. He looked around, trying to decide the right thing to do.

'He's just a phony!'

His whisper was as dry as the parched screen door. The age-old lock reviled him with its noise. Velocity can be viewed from any angle but the audience in the foreground may not be the best judge of the action on stage. The real hustlers are always backstage.

The bolt beat a boom into the darkness on the other side of the door. The door opened a crack and he slipped in, fingers wriggling on the wall for the switch. Sami needed to feel brave in those few moments of standing alone in the drowsy blackness. The tube light flickered like a mad grin.

Then scraps of a face.

A body in a pile of torso, arms and legs.

Insomniac eyes.

Particles of an unvoiced presence.

Boldness abandoned Sami. The long tube light shrank into a short stub. Its industry of light contaminated by the intensity of stark nakedness. Was it the eyes, the face or the body that was bare? Perhaps all of it. Whatever the case, he was no steward of salvation to match that guardian of transgression! Sami's contradictions began to mumble to him the most suitable courses of action. One of them was to turn and bolt, being a nimble man. He declined to do that. Defense lay in staying calm and not showing fear. The thought gave him some confidence.

24

'Yogesh?'

His voice was as soothing as his fear and the crouching figure in the corner was as bare as clarity. Before he could say anything else, it began to crawl away with its creepiness in tow. Sami did not move until the dark chimera had withdrawn completely into another room. The kitchen was a refuge into which Sami disappeared with his fear, fatigue and famishment. The soothing blue flame of the gas chulha warmed him and the untouched food. He laid the table for himself, encouraged by the aroma, dispelling the dismal air.

Life is livable with or without disaster was his motto and he zoomed in on his food with this thought when he was accosted by Yogesh, appearing out of nowhere like an annotation of the next episode. Apprehension has a taste. Its bulky morsel refused to go down Sami's badly cramped throat when he was greeted in the most normal of manners.

'Hello Mr. Shaun!'

Melodrama can never be a remedy. Sami attempted adding to it by answering the greeting.

'Hello.'

Yogesh's articulate shadow crept up on the opposite chair.

'Would you like to eat?'

A thin echo of his voice returned to him, sucking all other sounds of the room.

'I'll get you a plate.'

And seeking tenuous diversion in that, he jumped out of his seat and brought him a plate. The globe lifted itself on its keel as Yogesh sat down at the other end of the table and pulled the plate in front of him. He would prevail over the soup. He would subjugate the stew. He would sustain what Sami prayed to dispel. He looked almost enlightened, possessed with a completely new idea.

'How are you feeling Mr. Samuel Shaun?'

He served himself, almost abetting the food to come to him.

'I am fine. How are *you* today?'

Sami studied the conflict of expressions on Yogesh's face.

'I am very pleased.'

He sensed a touch of trouble.

'With what?'

Yogesh answered that with only a smile which nurtured further worries.

'So, how come you decide to have dinner with me tonight?'

He felt like a captive before his question was answered.

'Who knows, maybe, it is your last night….' Yogesh's smile widened with his words.

Sami would have squealed at this but for the food in his mouth. The brothers-in-law blocked each other's thoughts with a stare. One blank with the amount of shock in it. The other, fresh. Fresh with new insight.

Yogesh completed his statement.

'….with me.'

'Oh!'

And Sami swallowed the already long lost morsel in his mouth and became meditatively clumsy for the rest of the dinner and considered clearing the table as quickly as possible while Yogesh sat, watching Sami sweat it out. Yogesh continued to sit at the dining table, sharpening the spotlight on himself while Sami made preparations for another night of, hopefully, uneventful sleep. He was already behind his schedule of remote dreams and rusty snores and told Yogesh, the facilitator of darkness, to switch off the lights when he went to bed.

'The lights are already off.'

Yogesh nodded at the good deal of black ink now queued up in the wings. And so the history of that house in Lal Kothi began to blend with the fiction of Yogesh that night.

25

Sami would be unfit to forget it as long as he would live in it. Sleep flattened him immediately on his bed and the mind's spotlights were lit and the curtain lifted on the stage of the final drama even as an incognito band of several creatures began to play their muses' vessels. Nimble shades of no acclamation appeared and pretended a resemblance to something else. The dysphoria of woes was their tale. Their songs interfaced with the sounds of bleakness. And they were arrayed in the vintage costumes of long neglected learning. Like that of death. Dust to dust. Ashes to ashes.

The implications thawed the deep sleep into thin substance. When the last act unfolded, wits turned to witlessness with insinuations of petrification, delivered in gibberish idioms and metaphors. Night divided itself. The hour struck like conditioned enlightenment. Sami's eyes opened and a long scream froze in his throat.

Hovering over him was a polished countenance, carved out of rubbery night. A pair of soapy eyes, shone in their center like shots of melting wax.

'Yogesh!'

Sami's clammy whisper was like a cue because the very picture of adverse fate, vanished immediately like a swindler's trick. He swung out of the bed and switched on the light and went to the little room. Yogesh was fast asleep.

'Yogesh! Yogesh!!' He called out softly.

There was no response. He returned to his bedroom and sat down on the edge of the bed. His body craved more sleep but the eyes would not close.

The morning played a waiting game and when at last it arrived, he wasted no time and gave Yogesh the money to go back to the Province of Ignorance. They did not indulge in the polite jargon of sentimental farewells. One's indifference matched the other's desperation. The only thing common was their well concealed loathing for each other. Yogesh packed up his two suitcases. Sami felt it was his duty to explain something.

'You will have to change the train at........'

Yogesh turned and spoke from his anecdotal frame.

'Destinations are always undisclosed.'

Sami opened his mouth again but he was already out of the door.

'I can drop you to…....'

He turned away from his unfinished offer. There was a greater task to be accomplished immediately.

'I was afraid...'

The graphic details of the night penetrated Charu's imagination and she heard him out without interruption on the phone.

'I don't know what his intentions were!'

At the end, he still sounded breathless.

'Nothing! It is plain. He just wanted to go back.'

She said it but she felt stumped. Cheated.

'What wrong did we do?'

Perhaps some inconvenient truth was playing hide and seek with them.

'We tried our best.'

But she remained uninspired.

'Inform mother,' she instructed.

Meaninglessness never motivated her.

'Inform her that he has left for her home.'

It was Ray's domain.

'I will.'

Inexact worlds frustrated her.

'Bye!'

She was filled with placid chagrin and he with guileless adolescence and a potent grunt. Sometime later she inconvenienced him with her nagging and asked him if he had informed mother.

'Yes I did.'

Indeed, he had. He had carried out her instruction to the *letter*, that is, he had written a *letter* to his mother-in-law.

It reached her after one week.

26

Yogesh was simply another nonentity in the numbing confines of the general compartment. The long exhausting journey made him realize his potential to be human again. Gradually, the passengers edged into his thoughts and he pieced together their saga from their conversation, which was definitely more enriching than his own nebulous epic. He surrendered to their babble. Submitted to their proximity. And even resigned to their food.

He reciprocated to their humanness in small ways. Like conceding room to the newcomers. Allowing a dozing head to dispose itself on his shoulder. Fetching water for a child at nondescript stations. Giving his approval by a nod and a smile to the general rant. In the end, he was affected by the myth of existence. The superstition of life. The fable of the world.

He surrendered to the feeling and a long time passed like tradition. He was thankful for the great expedition into ignorance. It is one of the purest forms of adventure. Until the great station swung into view. A signboard bore the legend: *City of Constantia*. His face lit up like a jar of fairies.

A withering trail transfigured into an inflamed *Private Road*. The saga of psychotic, hysterical insanity into an allegory of spiritual battle. He stepped out and began walking with rapid steps. The exit welcomed him to resume his rudderless quest. He hired a rickshaw.

'Constantia.'

Soon crossroads of asphalt passed into the boulevards of the brain. The propensities of the heart. The proclivities of the soul.

The wide, tumultuous sewer of the city road ended and the bottleneck of the *Private Road* led into the quietly oozing desert of the Fairy Dale. The sky was white with immaculate heat and under it, Constantia choked in its austere sauce, rising above the wrinkled up moss. He did not go through the white gate but made his way outside, through the bushes to the corner house.

Like a picture in profile, it looked back at him, subdued by the new occupants. The long sticks of the Amaltash stirred like epic tongues of ethereal breeze and the Khajoor beat its fronds in the language of nowhere. The servants, stiff with the starch of sweat, watched him.

He retreated into the shade of the prehistoric *imli* tees. Time lingered longer on their bark and in their secret hollows, day disappeared and changed into the costumes of dusk. Dewy traps of moonlight dripped into the misty eyes of the creatures of darkness and washed away the indolent dirt of the day from their brows and they played out games of the decoy perils of night's many webs. He took a tour of the long coast of the night and sat down beside the river. And interpreted each eyeful jewel of the deep sky.

27

A critically long 'ohffooo…' immediately drew Aru's attention. It was an eloquent sound which Victoria only made once in five to ten years. Aru, who had by now become the great arbiter of all her mother's affairs, took the letter without so much as an 'excuse me or may I, and read it in equal disbelief. Alphabetical possibilities from a to z lined up in their minds. Sami went into a state of denial when he heard Victoria's voice at the other end of the receiver.

'No, no, no….,' he tried to score some self-defense by repeating that single word.

'Why didn't you call us up as soon as he left you?'

Aru took the phone.

'Tell Didi that Yogesh has not reached us.'

Sami did not want to finish the conversation.

'I will….'

The gravity in his voice increased on account of his distress at that injunction and befittingly Charu ground him into powder with extremely rough articulation after which she called up mother.

'What is to be done?' She sounded aghast.

A woman's intuition may abandon her sometimes.

'I have written to Ray to come over.'

But not a mother's.

'We will together find him.'

And coupled with her profound faith it made Victoria invincible.

'Hmmm.'

Charu admired her indomitable force.

'Tell me if I can help in any way.'

'Hmmm.'

The alternating hmmms were an inconclusive endorsement to end the conversation.

28

A withering sense of decay gripped Ray. The letter from Victoria was brief in its details about Yogesh's vanishing act. At the end it said *Come soon. Your loving Ma.*

Where could he be? He muttered and made preparations with great speed. The jostling crowds of Mehrauli choked the blue line bus heading for the ISBT but he managed to get a window seat. He was suddenly possessed by inconclusive feelings of love for the undying race of ragged apparitions, lying on the pavements like inactive freak pictures. His restless imagination scanned their faces and forms. It would be easy to catch sight of Yogesh's dynamism among them. Like an answer to an unasked question, the distance between him and his brother assumed an ambiguity. Except for the clang of the journey, there was a blurred silence that he carried from the dusk of the day into the dawn of the night with bundles of sleep rolled up under each eye.

The Province of Ignorance was still unready when he swung through it and stood before the house with the pipal tree. Someone peeped out of a door in the Teacher's Row. He ignored the curious gaze. He knew, they knew that the doing of the surreal was fixed forever in their lives and yet its collusion with their real, material existence could not be excused as a figment of imagination. The latch on the door was a chain of many links. He held it but the door was not bolted from inside. He was expected.

The house was silent like a gagged slug. The mediocrity of sleepy dogs, Zella among them, and scratchy hens was unavoidable but Victoria hummed over it all with a hovering divine canticle. The only other thing that matched it was Aru's guilelessness. Victoria had some soothing news.

'He has been seen in the City of Constantia around the Anglican church and the GPO.'

Ray fidgeted with the prefix of a haunting excitement.

'Let's go immediately.'

Fresh memories of a transcendent time, rambled on in his head. They took the day train next day armed with an elemental black and white photograph of Yogesh that coalesced the present and the past into a moody delusion.

'Should we go to your Perfect Aunt's house?'

The restrained journey turned neither left nor right.

'No. We will accomplish this thing and return home by the evening.'

Sustained determination of one.

'Yes. Why should she be unnecessarily bothered?'

And determined sustenance of the other.

'We will go to the GPO area first.'

The absence of debate between mother and son brought the journey straight to the point. The unknown hankered after them from the station as they made a passage through the late afternoon already inflating into a paleness. An exceptional coordination of Providence with their passionate search, brought them face to face with the very man who would know anything about anything or anyone.

The Tea Man of GPO.

He was so entangled between casual customers and vital bystanders that it seemed only natural that he should have been directly approached.

29

The General Post Office and the Anglican Church resonated with the sounds of the wide road that passed between them but the lives of those who crouched in the shadows of these two buildings did not catch the vibrations. Both buildings were part of the City's business hub, *Hazmatganj* but the two façades rejected each other's symbolism. The gothic sacredness of one and the sacrilegious coarseness of the other.

The Tea Man was patient with both as he redressed each of his customer's concerns with neutral dexterity. Profit could never be the concern of such liberality.

The day was past its climax and he, a sharp judge, knew without so much as looking at the two people that they were about to approach him but not for his tea.

'Hello.'

Without any disdain, he let that pass and the man with the photograph did not feel slighted. The man with the photograph touched his arm. It was like a ceremony. It was expected. The Tea Man stopped everything and turned and looked sublimely at the man who had touched him. Ray was astounded by the symmetry of the man's features. It was like looking into the face of someone who would stop to help anyone on any road, anywhere. He asked his question.

'Have you seen this person?'

The divine is not a Levite but a Good Samaritan. The Tea Man looked at the photograph with his dazzling eyes and said yes in his magnificent voice, nodding at the photograph.

'Yes, I know him.'

Immediately Ray knew that he was looking at his brother's saviour.

'When he arrived here, I helped him find employment.'

In those moments Ray saw the profane and the spiritual competing with each other to expand their range.

'He would leave his suitcases with me.'

Both crossed into each other's zones.

'While he would go and pull other people's weight.'

In so doing, they gave birth to phantoms.

'Now he is living somewhere else in the city.'

Wraiths that haunted both the sides.

'He still comes to have tea at my stall.'

Ray had a prevision of those phantoms.

'He is a very good man.'

They would haunt him until he would sit down and write their story.

30

'Will he come today?'

Ray looked around hoping to see Yogesh emerge out of the afternoon.

'It's Sunday today. He will come only to have tea at my stall. And whenever he does, he gives me extra money.'

But the brightness remained empty.

'I say to him, bhaiyya, what have I done for you?'

Ray always carried with him a partnership of paper and pen.

'Whatever good we can do for others. Who knows?'

They scratched together to form words of a brief letter.

'But he only says, "keep......"'

'When he comes,' Ray interrupted him, 'please give him this. I am his brother. She is his mother. We have been looking for him.'

The critical scholar of humanity, took the piece of paper, looked at it lingeringly and tucked it away safely.

'He must have become 'naraaz' over some matter and left home. Such things do happen.'

The rationale for any further conversation was tapering towards a conclusive end. Ray took out some money.

'Here, please keep this.'

He held it gingerly as if afraid the Tea Man might reject it as implied insult.

'No, no. Please…. I cannot accept this…'

But Ray did not want to miss the chance to be good to the man who had been overwhelmingly good to his brother.

'This is just to say, "thank you!"'

And he deftly pushed it into his pocket and then they left.

Ray turned once to look at the Tea Man but he was back to his agenda of serving humanity without any biases.

'Should we go to my sister's house? We can spend the night there and come here the next day.'

Victoria's intuition seemed to be giving up but Ray's was picking up.

'But why? When he gets the note he will head straight for the station, you will see.'

He felt no attraction for the City of Constantia.

'We must leave immediately.'

Victoria was not so sure.

31

They returned to the Province of Ignorance and waited for the letter to accomplish a reverse loop of events. How quickly it did, caught them by surprise. There was a knock on the door, next day. Ray opened the door, a short distance from where he was sitting in the courtyard but the person who stepped into the house was from some unknown part of the infinite universe. The face was thin and tanned and the body lean but in the centre of his closely cropped head, at the back, was a long thin wisp of hair which poised like a lead title.

'Yogesh! You got the letter!!'

Ray held and kissed him.

'Yes!'

The default deadline of love had been reached.

'And you came!!'

They stood like itching statues in a passionate embrace.

'I have a mother and brother!'

Ray felt on his own cheek too, the parched lips of a long lost relationship.

'I could not wait any more.'

Victoria came out and Aru stagnated behind her.

'I had to see my mother and my brother.'

Ray let go of him and they too swayed in the seizures of Yogesh's oblivious rediscovery.

'The Tea Man is my friend.'

He could not stand for long at the crossroad of damp eyes.

'He told me, "Your mother and brother came. They are very good people. They gave me money."'

And sat down, still pursued by his journey.

'I was very happy. You honored my friend.'

32

The physical resemblance to the old Yogesh was coincidental. He appeared more like an earthen vessel still spouting chaste English.

'You will be staying for a few days. Right?'

Victoria wanted to cherish those unfamiliar moments a bit longer.

'No, no. I teach English to a group of students and must return to them tomorrow.'

While Ray inched closer to him and touched his arm.

'Where?'

He did not dodge the intimacy.

'At the University hostel. I stay there.'

Curiosity whirled around with more questions.

'How did that happen?'

Questions that were not compliments.

'I'll tell you…'

Answers that were only supplements.

'Tell us from the beginning.'

Afternoon had overtaken the late morning.

'I will.'

Victoria made him a lovely vegetarian lunch.

'I must tell you that I appreciate the effort you have put in preparing this meal. I have not had such good food in a long time.'

He looked up from the plate, his head looking as small as a prehistoric sample and whenever he moved it, the strand of hair danced like a hopeful on top of it. His eyes circulated like great scholars in the tiny skull.

'The Tea Man helped me a lot but the priest was no less. After the hard heat and dust of the day's work, I spent the cool nights in his temple in the shadow of the GPO, opposite the church. He was a kind old man. We lay under the soft stars and he told me pauranic stories.'

Time and history were dealing with each other's feuds of rewards and punishments.

'In this way, I earned my bread.'

Like curses of a father. Some of them proven correct.

Dar, dar ki thokre khaoge…

Some of them disproven.

Theekra le ke bheek mangoge….

Unconscious echoes of the past overcame conscious reflections of sanity while Yogesh continued his saga.

'One day, I was ferrying two young men across the city to the university hostel.'

A weakening wave crossed the story teller's brow.

'I heard them discussing me.'

He needed to yawn.

'One of them, a student leader at the university, asked me, "You seem to be from a good family! Are you educated?"'

But Ray, his listener, would not allow a single break in the narrative.

'I answered in the affirmative. They asked to see my certificates. I carried them with me. They were amazed. "Distinction in matriculation! ISC, BSc!! Come with me, you can stay in the hostel and do tuitions!"'

The teller, drained, dithered between adjournment and adjustment.

'That's what I did until the Tea Man, my friend, gave me your letter.'

He chose the latter and grabbed a moment of silence by handing Ray a sheet of paper, crumpled like mortality.

> *Dear brother Yogesh,*
> *How are you? Please come home. We are worried about*
> *you. We love you.*
> *Your mother and brother.*
> *Teachers' Row*
> *Province of Ignorance*

His dark eyes moved from face to face like a moth trying to enter the window panes of light.

'It is true. There is so much love here.'

Ray ignored its plight, his window opening only to ask questions.

'Why do you have a chhoti on your head?'

And then closed cautiously.

'That I kept after the suddhhikaran ceremony.'

Potent light remained uninclined to reflect on the profane.

'That happened after they declared that as my forefathers were Hindus, I should have a ghar vapasi, my return to the fold.'

And obstructed by the mundane.

'I cook my own food but have to share everything with the boys in the hostel. I pay them for all their help.'

33

In a mother, however, plenty originates with light. She gives birth to plenty with the unencumbering agony of joy. Victoria went to the market in the evening and bought him many things. Some of them were: A trunk as a repository for his fortune's portion. A stove to light temporal fire. Pots and pans to rival his contention with the world. The steady wisdom of underclothes. And bed linen to mend sleep.

He retired early into his night in the veranda. His bed had been made there on his request. Ray sat at the huge dining table in the tiny room, doped in the ink of his night's words. Zella was under it, in her own part of the night, alert to the existence of the twisted legions of darkness around the house. Aru and Victoria were in their beds in adjacent rooms, feeling a fresh stealth in their nights' prowl.

Sleep appeared slowly like the departed. Lifeless. Lost. Nonexistent. But vanished at the first sound from the veranda. First it was like a drain pipe, coldly erupting with a trickle. Zella sat up and Ray cocked an ear, a trick he had learnt from his ancient pet long ago. Aru opened one eye and Victoria an ear. Then it gained force.

Zella got up. Ray stood up. Aru opened both eyes and Victoria both ears. And then it unfastened into a vast torrent. Zella wagged her tail sympathetically at Aru who came and stood near Ray and wept. Victoria went and stood near Yogesh; the blue New Testament, a living thing, in her hand. She touched his forehead, it was hot with the delirium of dreams, and said an anxious prayer that was perhaps cut off on the edge of nightmares.

She placed the book near his pillow but they had to surrender to trauma's time frame, which for them was only one night but Yogesh must languish in it, in an endless climax of many days.

Morning found him fettered by a fever. Victoria went to the Province's practicing pioneers of medicine and got him a reviving dose.

'You need rest and care.'

Her impartial hand caressed his forehead.

'No, I must leave today. My students will suffer.'

Love restrains but his quest liberated him from it.

'Ray, accompany your brother till his hostel. Settle him down.'

But Ray was no deliverer. He too was on the run.

'Of course!'

With a predictable measure of hesitant willingness in his voice, he agreed to embark on the journey to the City of

Constantia with Yogesh. The train dubbed him a coward. Its refrain sang its unfriendly song which got on his nerves.

You abandoned your father.

The tracks chased him.

You will abandon your brother.

He looked at him. The journey was draining Yogesh.

'You must eat something.'

He needed to be released from it.

'I am all right.'

Yogesh bravely looked at the full berths. The calculations of Ray's mind were like those multitudes. Nurturing the self. He was an elite renegade.

And a low rat.

34

Yogesh's cross loomed in the distance, dusty, coarse and hollow. He would be nailed to it again soon enough. There was no escaping it. Ray could not see it and even if he could he would have nothing to do with it. He held his brother by an arm and led him out of the congested station.

The sooner I get this over with....

There was nothing to prop him up on the tonga. Yogesh kept swaying from side to side with every impartial bump in the road. His journey was unrelenting. Food was only a coincidence.

'You must eat....'

Unlike Ray, it was not a remedy for Yogesh. By his calculation, this concert did not need abetment but abandonment. He was surprised by his own agility once they reached the university hostel. The room was as empty as the stage of a melodrama. Out of its neat emptiness emerged a roommate and Yogesh, who could barely stand and walk, introduced them to each other.

Ray made the bed on a string cot. Yogesh inaugurated it and was served the packed food. There was nothing more filling than Victoria's victuals but all the new things she had given, tried to annex the room's emptiness. The roommate, a source of the emptiness, watched Yogesh who lay on his bed in the center in his heap of possessions as on a newly discovered but tiny island. Ray was qualified to feel some pity for both. Yogesh expressed a wish to bathe. The toilets were at the back. No bathroom but an open place with a well and a hand pump on a cemented block. No light too.

'I bathe here daily, early in the morning.'

He walked now all by himself. After the bath, he lay down again under a weak bulb. The light outside had turned the complexion of devalued currency. If he was lucky, Ray could get the late evening train back to the Province. Yogesh sensed his urgency.

'You can leave, I'll be fine.'

'Are you sure? I can stay if you want.'

'I will be looked after.'

He looked at his roommate who had inched closer to the periphery of Yogesh's sparkling new world. Ray bent and kissed him and hurried out of the indulgent desolation.

Misery cannot be postponed and it cannot be neutralized. The triumph of misery is that it forfeits one of everything in the end. Fear it and the best advice under such circumstances is to run from it. Hence, a trivial rickshaw. Followed by a hurtling train. In its cramped general compartment, Ray the coward, spun through his fresh haunting memories of a burdensome brother. Lastly, look impassive. People are greatly influenced by an impassive face. It passes for strength and courage. It even becomes the hall mark of eminence. Ray looked as impassive as disbelief.

The house in the Province of Ignorance stood awake at one thirty am. Victoria and Aru sat at the huge dining table in the tiny room and confronted him, the former with her patient silence and the latter with her impatient questioning. Ray tended to both at the same time with his sophisticated descriptions and explanations but only thickening worry seemed to grow on their brows.

'The boy he is sharing the room with is very helpful.'

And Ray was done for the day with that last bit of reassurance. The rest of the night was loaded with Aru's final, concluding remarks. She was the master of dictation and the boss of command though Victoria still deceived herself with the notion that she was the mother. Ray bothered himself briefly with the flawless notions of both as he attached himself to a slightly modified sleep. After the lights were put out, sleep rested like bails on the wickets of the pitch black night. Somewhere in the game of darkness, Zella scratched an avalanche of crumbling fur, making the gloom fuzzy. Like her memories. She still, however, responded to the uncertain night with agility. Still meek and gentle, modest and obscure like a true pet should be.

35

The space around Yogesh irradiated with his mother's riches for some time and kept away that associate of sickness called Emptiness. The Emptiness of the room. The Emptiness of the slowly inching forward roommate. Of the lone yellow bulb. The desolate corridors. But how long could a mother's blessings hold out? Defeat was finally conceded, the last ones to be spared for the time being, were only those things that were under him: namely, the mattress, the bed sheet and the pillow. As he relapsed, the choreography began. A rehearsal in the form of a borrowing. And then the final. As his waned, the infinite arm of depredation waxed. He was glad: At least somebody was benefitting. In fact, he granted it.

'Just take me to my 'mother.''

'Oh yes, you have a home.'

'A loving brother and a mother.'

'No, no. My 'mother' is Kathy Damyanti.'

He gave them the address of her house in another city close to the City of Constantia. So off they sent him to this other 'mother'. Hungry, sick and destitute, he arrived at her doorstep.

36

Sagacity had made a permanent abode in Kathy Damyanti's thin face and it affected the way she expressed supreme happiness and supreme sorrow as she hugged and kissed the young man who kept calling her 'mother'.

'But I am not your mother.'

Belief and fiction circumvented her caress by turns.

'I am your phoophee. Your mother lives in the Province of Ignorance.'

By no persuasion could the shrunk face provoke much love in her bosom now.

'You are my mother.'

She had coveted this child long ago but Bonny had declined.

'Poor Bonny's son,' she mumbled.

She had made her peace with that.

'Write to Victoria.'

The philosopher, Anthony Sahani, entered the scene, looking more enlightened than ever.

'Bonny's son! Bonny's son!' She kept reviving her brother's memory with tears to her husband's cool disregard.

'I am not your mother. Victoria is.'

Yogesh began to crumble. He did not call her 'mother' again, though, she would have got used to it. She wrote to Victoria who arrived as soon as she got the letter. He was too weak to resist. The credible part was that he went with her. Destiny had reached the last chapter. Victoria knew the drill. She began his treatment for the last time. She had the sanction to be brave.

37

Tranquility returned to his soul in the psychiatric ward once again. The detour would have its consequences. Circular revival was no revival. The consciousness was disturbing. The lose edge was back and he tried in vain to shrink away from it. Light evaded him and darkness had only disdain for him. Victoria's visits during her holidays repulsed him. His docile and healthy looks buried his scorn well. The friction was too much but he was discharged.

'You are a new man.'

The doctor believed in the hope of renewal but his caution was not new.

'Do not discontinue the treatment yourself, Mrs. Deut.'

She believed in redemption.

'I hope his condition is fixed.'

The doctor did not dispute her hope and belief.

'I hope so too.'

Heaven allows hurt and loss but that is its way of combating hell.

'What is God's will is difficult to tell.'

She affirmed her faith with a sigh.

A purposeless life is also very spiritual. It is claimed fully by the unseen. There is no refund. The skill is to guide it gently onward towards the end of its purposelessness. Give it secure cover. Do not be misled into believing that it can be abandoned. Victoria knew all this intuitively. Only Aru felt that the responsibility was immense and took it upon herself to handle it her way. So the shadows got together into augmenting themselves around him. Old prejudices became bold and sprang like tigers upon their prey.

38

A remote consciousness kept working against the safeguards of the medicines. Unlike them, it was not that easy to swallow life whole. The only respectable standard in the Province of Ignorance was gossip. The Deut family presented a shocker regularly to maintain that standard. People of the Province had penetrating insight even into a coma. The obvious things were the most secretive ones. Even God became visible at such times as they attributed to Him people's sufferings as long overdue dividends for their sins. A super swell in the garb of sympathy warranted the questions.

'How is he?'

Then explicit pity.

'Poor fellow!'

And finally manifest insolence.

'What a life!'

Victoria's superiority in such matters to stay over and above them smothered them all in no time except of course, Yogesh's own shades of grey and black. So he lay like the landscape, biding his time, until such time, when he would be able to append dilapidation to himself like a final blow or something. He lay in bed the whole day and night, while Victoria's countenance rose over him with the sun during the day and the moon at night, coaxing him to come for the meals or to go out for exercise or to perform little chores.

He did not resist Aru's explosiveness. She did not need provocation to make one feel the tremor of her iron rule. And therefore, her new protégé, Shayna, the adopted child of the Imperfect Aunt [an exact opposite of the Perfect Aunt] arrived to be taught, trained and disciplined by her. Charu's children, having been taught and disciplined, had safely fluttered away.

39

The only person who experienced life's rush was Ray. The pace of his life had still not spent his concern for Yogesh and hence he toured the Province of Ignorance during his holidays. He seemed to have found temporary redemption in a gadgetry jumble. The transistor, an old friend from the City of Constantia was now accompanied by a cassette player and a synthesizer.

BBC's top of the hour signature tune futilely stabbed the solitude of the house. Its news flashes beamed into the gloom and ceased to be. The tinsel twinkle of the world events dimmed before the gloom's flawless uniformity. He presented the synthesizer to Yogesh.

'You taught me a little bit.'

His smile was a sanction for Yogesh to touch and hold it.

'Play something.'

Erased memories of an acoustic piano surprised the house. Zella used her last reserves of strength to freeze as his fingers tried to pick up a long forgotten passionate path on the limited keyboard. But it was the cassette player which turned his memory into a musical smudge. The Bees. Tragedy tragedy they sang.

But their tragedy had a tempo and he could not be won back to their tempo of tragedy again. So Ray let it go and left to continue on his voyage, armed with his transistor, synthesizer and his cassette player. The sap must be prolonged at any rate, somewhere else.

The plain little girl, Shayna, was one of the many shadows in that house. Slow shadows that even the brightest sunlight found difficult to lift. They laid a subtle siege around Victoria's fortified city. In no hurry, they encamped, dark and leisurely, tranquil and passive under the guava and the custard and the peach and the papayas. The huge red croton plants lent them their redness so that they looked like patches of dry curdled blood.

In the back courtyard too, the shadows danced undisputedly day and night. In the vegetable patches, they assumed a cultivated allure which saved them from being weeded out by Victoria. The birds descended from the pipal and serenaded in the trees with them and in their unchanging subtleties, the squirrels sued and wooed each other. Their dithering waves kept Yogesh asleep and awake.

Once upon a time he had been a shadow trainer but now he hung on to them like a detachedly attached leaf. While Aru balanced herself on a different limb altogether. The course of her life had always taken a rival position to that of Yogesh: She was in the love lane. Its asphalt led to the cobblestones of her future husband, Sunny's house, with whom she was always either trying to end or resuscitate the affair. For either purpose, she used, without any scruples, Shayna as her messenger girl who became privy to all the little exchanges between them with teasing little notes bearing pressing details of heart broken feelings. Soothing requests for rough meetings.

They had a pedestrian approach to 'the whole thing' and over time 'the whole thing' lost its radiance of romance until finally what was left of it could only be mistaken for sublimity. It made Shayna immune to all kinds of love: romantic, familial, platonic, agape…. She began to hate the sight of her mother, the Imperfect Aunt but ultimately, she became immune to hate as well. Life did not obsess her at all. Not even death. Her father, the Imperfect Uncle passed away suddenly and everyone thought her awkward when they looked hard under the surface for signs of unspent tears but failed to find any.

40

Autumn brought blurred messages for the spent spirits. Yogesh sat under a shower of softly falling leaves.

'Read your Bible, beta.' Victoria encouraged him.

Which he did and for as long as he read the Bible, the precious piercing of hands and feet of the divine invested him with holy passion but as soon as he put it aside, the empty, terrestrial shadows hoarded around him. Like Zella, resigned to stay under the table and the beds, he remained in a corner of the house like a faintly extinguished light. But Victoria would not have it.

'You must sometimes go out of the house, beta.'

She believed that beside her faith, he needed a change of air to make his recovery possible. He went out, the inner turmoil deadlocked with the exterior of peace and calm. A blue-vein stagnation unlike Aru's arterial red rage. With eyes like uncut diamonds, his placid appearance could inspire a generation of venerated saints. In the church, the three of them did give the impression of a restored portrait when they stood together with Victoria in the center, singing an English hymn; the atmosphere moderated by the dry density of their audience's spirituality.

The dryness served a purpose. It made them more resilient than meek. Resilient to deep spirituality. Resilient to a true hunger and thirst for God. There they dwelt behind their doorways, adding nothing to no one outside but building their empires of conjecture and raising their children, the very pupae of ignorance within the borders of those. Their comprehension of existence buttressed their refusal to surrender to mainstream imagination. And so Yogesh absorbed their full interest when he perched on an elevated root of the pipal tree, that radar of revelation, and began to consider the preexistence of nothingness with songs. The beginning of his vanishing had begun, the end not yet in sight.

Innovation of eccentricity always draws a coarse audience. They first surrounded him with a very serious disregard. Eulogy in the vernacular can be intriguing but as he sang with the charm of foreboding, they began to applaud with sighs. The avatar of radical glory fermented their thirst to put their own life's yarns into songs. The sullen magnum opuses of Kishore Kumar interpreted the chronicles of their lives. The epic recitals of one song stood out among the others. It soothed their own wilting tunes. Their own life's waning. It wore down the world's wisdom. The song that articulated so much sweet languishing was:

Mera jeevan kora kaagaz, kora hi reh gaya.....

The sound of this anthem of emptiness diffused and dissolved far and wide, waking up spirits of infinity, who blind with insomnia drew like unhurried moths and tenuously clutching this sad new flame, sucked the thin air of its echoes and were thus one by one liberated and sent thankfully to their sheer ends.

41

The apostles of conspiracy and subterfuge, however, desecrated the worship with baleful contemplations. They remembered.

'Wasn't he the one who visited this place with his younger brother?'

'Like some foreign evangelist!'

'And preached to us!!'

They mentioned him like a refrain in their conversations.

'And now look at him!!!'

Aru was an immortal of convention. A fanatic of clichés. A perpetuator of wrinkles. Quite the opposite of Victoria.

'Why do you send him out of the house? People talk.'

For whom innovation was a custom.

'They ask him awkward questions.'

The heir of a richer and superior emotional heritage.

'Let them. At least he is busy.'

Aru did not inherit any of it.

'He sings funny songs.'

She became white like a sore knuckle.

'They laugh at him.'

Sending him out was a breach of rules. Her rules. Her consent had to be taken. She armed herself with the licence to take a slow toll on Yogesh's cooling stew.

His medicine was no match to it.

There was no clash but the one way confrontations did twist the mind's oscillations and he stayed more and more out of the house to avoid her. Though she was right, in a way, that he should not have been allowed out, the shuddering thought of another shroud as yet did not cross anybody's imagination. In fact, it was Victoria who muzzled all such thoughts.

'You are like your father,' she said to Aru.

'It is an unfair comparison,' Aru replied.

And so, over this matter of Yogesh, the two could not be reconciled. In all this Shayna and Zella remained silent like unmarked graves.

42

He was called to exact suffering. It was a harsh cause. The channel strange and the force intensely disturbing. Wasted young men as well as the remitted ones surrounded him, scratching their heads to make him say something to them, pertinent or impertinent. He complied, sharing a slice of his passion with each one of them, the greater and the lesser, making them feel rich in their poverty. They didn't have to stand in a line for their share of his attention. He knew what was due to each one of them. His genuineness struck even the pseudo admirers off guard. They measured their nothingness with his fullness. The fullness he had achieved in the scorching heat of the City of Constantia's sun. It was in his eyes and face but it was more like when viewed from the depths of a pool. Sometimes he went away from them to be alone with his song.

Mera jivan kora kagaz…

The refrain could be heard from across the distant fields on the other side of the railway line. Sometimes they found him, reclining like an ornament on the mud bank along the track. That was when they began to sense his obsession for the train that went by Teacher's Row at five pm every evening. A mask reared itself in his face at its passing.

'Do you know where this train goes?'

They hustled a reply before it disappeared around the bend.

'To the City of Constantia.'

A storm of varied expressions passed over his face. The raiders of empty legacies tried again.

'The train slows down as it turns the corner of the football field.'

43

Substance can happen suddenly like God saying, 'Let there be light' and there was light. So one day, Ray walked through Victoria's indispensable empire, her almighty household. She was sitting in the backyard, like a colony chief among her hens and dogs, cutting up chaulayi. It is a huge culture in Teacher's Row, keeping coops and propping pens. The essence of a population can be caught on a Sunday.

The context of Ray's sudden visit was a photograph and the vocabulary a marriage proposal. Breathless and unambiguous, he presented the piece of thick paper like a bill of redemption, as if saying, *I need to be involved!* The girl in the photograph was neither a bewitching beauty nor was she washed in the gels of charm or embedded in cakes of cosmetics.

But her pupils were soaked in melting love.

The smoky hair floated around her face in turbulent anticipation.

The neck was approximate, followed by sensitive shapes.

The smile just right like an enchanting essence of peace.

The teeth were like neglected verse.

The last bit was what Victoria judged people by and eons of studied silence passed before she spoke.

Ray was like a repetitive adolescent.

'She is nice! Is she nice?'

She only uttered a longwinded resonance.

'Hmmm.'

He looked at the picture again.

'What is it?'

His confidence was a little mangled.

'Is it what, Ma??'

But only pawns piss on the roadside. Like an empress, she was never sudden with anything verbal.

'Ma, what it is???'

Aru came like a diversion and took the picture.

'Ohhhhooooo!'

That was her way of showing fierce admiration.

'I like her. What is her name?'

'I call her Candy.'

She was judge, jury, executioner and a great advocate.

'Candy is pretty, Ma.'

Yogesh too came and stood quietly at a little distance, attracted by all the acceleration and caught a glimpse of the evidence in the chief counsel's hand.

'Good job, Ray.' Aru beamed, now preoccupied with the photograph. She could control and guide everything in that house including, in most matters, Victoria's will. Zella meandered through the house like an aged delusion and came and stood near Ray who shot her a petty smile. Victoria got up and gave Ray an abidingly long but loving look.

'Only the teeth are a little crooked and twenty days is a very short notice for the wedding!'

44

In those twenty exceptional days, she put aside Yogesh and concentrated on bringing up the rear, that is, to release Ray from the indefiniteness of bachelorhood. She passed on the hysteria of his wedding to her youngest sister who was just right, that is, neither Perfect nor Imperfect. She lived in Delhi too and invested with stunning, cheerful ability her very backbone to let her beautiful home be subverted by the relatives.

The fortified wedding cake, which stood solidly on the seismic grounds of Ray's marriage to Candy, was arranged by her. Her younger son agreed to be fitted into the best man's shipshape suit. The just right uncle, her husband, who kept his just right distance, provided his car for the ride to and from the church. In all this, Yogesh was the number one specimen, trying his best to look undisguisedly excluded like a huge clot. To everyone, the suddenness of his younger brother's claim on such a big chunk of life seemed almost criminal.

'How can the youngest get married off when his elder two siblings are still bachelors?'

The stinging question reached Ray's ears too, thanks to the wedding acoustics. But what was at stake? No one could guess at the time. The makeshift marriage concealed the deeper issues. The freak founder of his marriage did not even turn up to bid his family a goodbye. They waited and waited.

'Where is my son? How is he?'

'He's just got married, Ma! He's busy!!'

Victoria prayed for him and boarded the bus and the feather of truth gently brushed them away. In this way, finally, the irrevocable thing was set into motion.

45

Unlike childhood, adulthood is a mirage. What makes adulthood a mirage, is its quest for security. Yogesh never wanted it. In fact it was being imposed on him. Victoria was exhausted by it. Aru reacted to it differently on different days. And Ray had just embarked it. His quest for security. For happiness. For adulthood. To him, therefore, life had always been very corporeal. His contract was always with the contemporary. For Yogesh, life was a vaulting flash. It went back and forth. Like a blade of grass. In disembodied air. Yielding and unyielding. Thin and thick. Frothing and fawning. Unlike his family, the minions of life, he was cut out for the grim reaper's scythe a little too early. From the beginning.

The wedding should have been a holiday of triumph but Victoria did not believe in faint evasive fronts, facile in their cries of celebration. She was aware of the shove of singleness beginning to turn the house into a cradle of grudges, granting shadows to turn the house colder than what the winter could. In this context of hysteria, Yogesh's grief-plan of achieving immortality was justified. Aru's apprentice, Shayna was a witness.

She saw the square things. The round things. The rectangular. The triangular. And the others. Devil's inheritance. Shapes of hell. Infiltrating and invading. Wriggling punishments from hades. Faces without grins. Grins without faces. Shades that passed in front of Yogesh one by one. In calm order. Sometimes redeeming. Sometimes in an uproar. Stubborn apparitions from memory's asylum.

He did not seek refuge from them but from the tombstones at the back of Teacher's Row to which the Mission Compound residents made constant expeditions. The archives on the stones made his confidence skin-deep.

In loving memory of Boniah Deut.

Ace traps, where even the soul receives moderate mutilation.

Born on 23 September 1934.

Where the body becomes a pawn.

Died on 9 June 1991.

Against immortal words.

I am the resurrection and the life....

He had never seen a dead body.

He that believeth in me....

But only from a distance.

Though he were dead....

From over the wall.

Yet shall he live.

Along the railway track. Lives that had surrendered themselves to death. Resigned to sickness. Relinquished by freedom. And always subordinate to the living.

It would be five pm soon.

46

It was the last day of his life in the Province of Ignorance. That day, Victoria saw him literally slump over the Bible. The door was open before him and late October breeze illuminated the house like a floodlight, highlighting his face between the Word and the wind. A sad slow church bell rippled through the Mission Compound, its dirge for a little boy who had been dispossessed of life a day before. Victoria, a portrait of condolence, appeared behind Yogesh.

'Beta, I am going to attend the funeral.'

He nodded from the depths of what seemed to be devotion and leaned out a pinch to see her disappear from view. He put the Bible down and went out of the house with hungry speed in the opposite direction and watched the funeral from over the wall along the track. Among the elements of death was the chief one, the shepherd in white, leading his flock to their paid graves. Behind him, came the gushing crowd, colleagues of death, holding high the safe deposit box of the lifeless body. The mourners emphatically mourned the end but never begged for a new beginning.

The grave's tenuous reception of the body was suddenly disturbed by the sharp rebuff of a whistle. The five o' clock train was approaching. Rumbling steel eclipsing earthy peace. Steam diluting tears. A wind vane danced atop the engine with blazes of Gahanna in its belly and pampered white candles in the churchyard. He chose the first. Escape was a palpable thing.

He crossed the track over the quaking ballast stones. The vegetation was beginning to go into a waltz even though the train slowed down at the bend. He began to run in the opposite direction towards the rear of the train, aware of the buoyant faces in open windows above. But the train was not a collaborator. It was passing him by. Evading him. Abandoning him. Betraying him to live through the ordeal of sympathy. The torment of empathy. The trial of antipathy.

He changed his direction, now running parallel, trying to grab hold of the handle bar of the last compartment but a shoe was becoming lose. The antics of a shoelace were turning his enterprise wobbly. His doom seemed more credible in an instant as he lost a foothold on the ballast and needed no persuasion to follow the laws of gravity. His ignorance in this matter was the greatest as compared to all other matters. That is, the matter of death. He was not prepared for it.

He fell. Sharp pieces of rocks seized his right temple. Immediately, an erratic bright light overtook him, the prize he had been so long after. The inheritance of a purely spiritual existence. His muscles began to relax. Why did he have to try so hard for it?

47

His body found refuge between the ballast and the mud bank. His right eye was no longer within the purchase of its socket and a red patch began to grow under it on the craggy ground. The train was always the first informer of the eventuality because it always stopped in the event of only an accident. The little crowd of mourners slowly turned their attention from one ruined life to another. A hyper individual ran to the house opposite the pipal tree and announced it to Shayna. She groped for words when Aru asked her what had happened.

'It's....'

A shock wave was spreading across the Mission Compound and Aru caught it from Shayna without her having to say anything at all. With magnified eyes and mouth she clutched her niece and fainted, seeking her portion of comfort in oblivion. The news reached Victoria almost like a digression and she began her gallery walk of deaths from the

churchyard to the railway track, confined within the arms of
fresh mourners coming out of the houses, confirmed in their
belief that the Deut family was obsessed with 'haadsaas.'
But she, on the contrary, was unaffected by their beliefs and
promoted unambiguous calmness with every step. Those
who had heard of it only, witnessed it that day.

'Yogesh.'

She bent and touched his shoulder.

'Yogesh.'

She called out to him as if he were in some hiding place.

Desolation is a river.

'Get up, beta.'

She stood on its edge.

'Get up now.'

On the edge of Yogesh's irreversible abyss.

'There's nothing there.' A voice of loss whispered to her.

Hands reached out and pulled her back. She was walked
to the house and met Aru who was recovering from the
dim state of unconsciousness. Frail Zella stood beside them,
looking much unredeemed, though for Shayna much of
all that would remain a perverse cliffhanger. After all,
havoc had brought about an indefinite number of holidays.
The manipulators, on the other hand, swung the focus to
themselves. Calls were made. A stir created. Silence observed.
Agitation maintained with overwrought mourning.

Added to that, on the fringes of the tragedy, was the
appearance of a cast of khaki clad men but they were drawn
away from the scene by the sheer influence of Mr. Raman
Prakash. Grappling with the dead could begin only when

the men in khaki were satisfied that it was an accident. Until then Yogesh would have to languish out in the open while the impatience of the living swelled up which they tried to vent with mournful gregariousness or gregarious mournfulness. It was difficult to tell which out of the two was a façade.

Detachment is not a reflex. It is conditioned. It was night when he was finally delivered into the hands of his detached restorers. First they brought him in, gently nestled in their arms and put him on a takhat in the courtyard. The left eye dangled out, like a poor reflection of a once radiant obsession of the staring sun. Next they secured deep darkness around them with copious amounts of alcohol and set to work with rabid euphoria.

Bottle after bottle. Hour after hour. Detached night was attached in layers and layers of bandaging. The mourners dozed off one by one. Conditioned sleep took a strange route. Dreams turned into fluff and flew about like ticklish wasps, stinging someone or the other back into the deathwatch. They became aware of the pertinent urgency of the restoration in the courtyard.

Some of them got up to have a preview of things but were taken aback by the depressed mirth which is the patent prize of men and quickly returned to the safety of pure sadness, the absolute genre of women. At last, the sun got into its eastern lane. The men were right behind it. As it rose over the boundaries of the Province of Ignorance, a ballooning deformity of bandaging followed it over his left eye and forehead. If that could be called achieving a haunting victory, then it was that and it would haunt them all for the rest of their lives.

48

The highway was as slow as a cosmic vein. Hence, ignorance kept pace with the two passengers on the UP Roadways bus. Ray and his Imperfect Aunt, the first two people to head towards the Province of Ignorance, had not been told that the accident had been fatal and yet the aunt's face was a model of funereal sadness while Ray's looked impotent like the uncomfortable and slow night.

The old bus sagged with their weak wills and the eyes opened and closed alternately with hope and apprehensions. Was it only an accident? Conjecture embraced the mind like an elastic band, stretching and stretching. A placid piss port, namely a roadside dhaabaa, came into view, offering its free air, water and standing-stretching ground. The bus stopped and the passengers, all of them incarnations of eccentricity, climbed out of their paid cramped stuffiness as if it were their past. The Imperfect Aunt swallowed a mud-cup of tea with a yawn. Ray sipped a couple of them, standing on the alien asphalt of the foreboding mounting night. The crew returned with sufficient levels of glucose in their veins to engage the bus into galactic sound and fury.

Speed *is* a definite buffer against the haunting coils of darkness and the nervous headlights reassigned indefiniteness to the far end of the journey. The Imperfect Aunt smothered the drone of the bus with her snores while Ray kept injecting a little folded sheet of paper with the primitive ink of despair. It was his way of seducing hope with abandon. In spite of it, night's shell cracked like an egg and the sun became visible over the egg white of the slowly brightening clouds. The yolk rested unbeaten on the horizon's rim.

Ignorance abandoned them when they reached the parochial pulia. They saw two things: A plain white shamiaana and unblemished white flowers. The former stretched like a principal endowment of death over the entrance of the house and the flowers huddled in bouquets of sorrow in the hands of nimble footed visitors. They braced themselves for the most unprepared moment of all: grieving, in which, one does not know whether one is seeking or giving relief. But that is what the oasis of kin is like. On their own, everyone is in a desert.

Untamed wailing induced the Imperfect Aunt from the door itself to proceed in quick time to Victoria who was at the center of the watering hole of grief but Ray's tears were blocked and his voice was locked even though he tried very hard to access at least a whimper or a whisper of emotional crash but wanton restraint held fast.

Weeping and crying, he had discovered after his marriage, were impulsive things. Acts of whim, in solitude. And in a gathering, contests. Ugly and arbitrary. He marveled at his inability to cry. Was it guilt? For guilt forms a dam, an earthwork. There is nothing to say when one knows one has a hand in it. Only the innocent weep. And the shrewdest hypocrites. Or those who have made it a profession.

49

Mr. J. Pal had been kindly making caskets for generations of Christians and came with his paraphernalia to begin his thankless job. The crust of constant sorrowing cracked with his pragmatic hammering. The nails crowded into the wood one by one. A vapor wound up from the ice slabs kept beneath Yogesh. The hours pushed. Charu and Sammy arrived. The former stiflingly surrendered to tears and the latter interfered in honest sorrow with trivial tears.

The hours pulled. Kathy Damyanti, the phoophee arrived, looking like a tranquilised mummy. Her philosopher husband's general look of enlightenment was replaced by a disdain-for-death gaze. Mr. J. Pal finished his work to fit the robust body and the women began their work to disguise the box. Black satin outside, its allure uniform, with shiny sleepless flowers and patterns. White satin inside like an essence into which Yogesh slowly sank or rather it sank into him and made him look vanilla fresh in his suit. One eye closed. The other open under the bandage, awake forever through the miasma of memory.

The chorus of charged hearts was growing in and outside the house. The Perfect Aunt with the Perfect Uncle arrived, their incompatibility to imperfection set aside for the moment. The church bell began its dying palpitations. The slow *tonn...tonn....*precipitated the arrival of the prosaic padre with the poetic pronouncements of Providence. Tear drops fell for the last time as family members bent to kiss the dead. The lid closed on the sophisticated aura of flowers and perfumes, ending Yogesh's affiliation to the living. His hangout with the dead had begun.

The box was the highlight of the evening as the crowd pressed close like an argument under it and carried it out. The house emptied like a pent up emotion. The priest led, reading deftly but unimaginatively, words of ominous wisdom.

Words of irrevocable, irrefutable truth.

> *To everything there is a season,*
> *and a time to every purpose under the heaven:*
> *a time to be born,*
> *and a time to die.....*

Though mostly, life incurs debt and death takes away profit, if at all any. The junction of death arrived. Sweat plowed across the foreheads of the pallbearers as they put down their burden.

It was five o' clock. The train to Constantia pitched around the corner. Its whistle rose in a heaving affiliation of the previous day's events. Its grating fused with the priest's words and produced an untamed version of its own. In fact, it critically ripped the whole range of vocabulary from the Province of Ignorance to the City of Constantia.

Ray stood on a reef and listened. Victoria, silent and empty, below him, listened. It was imprecise. Jumbled. Haywire. But in those few seconds, mother and son marked the anarchy in its message and then it passed them by like a winged effulgence. The reef below Ray's feet began to turn into a steady shower of earth, beginning to lock the dead in his grave. A fresh mound of earth rose up in no time next to Bonny Deut's grave. The candles and the flowers added a matte finish to another flawless funeral.

50

A sudden air of idleness and vacancy penetrated the house. Yogesh's debut death cast a profound opaqueness of thought over everyone. His clothes still lay in a grieving mess in a corner. Even things need to be liberated from the curse of life and death. Victoria held them out to Ray delicately.

'Beta, these need to be burned.'

He walked back to the graveyard and set fire to them on a pile of dry weeds and then ventured over to the wall overlooking the railway track. A dog stood sniffing the accident spot. Ray climbed over the low wall and chased the dog away. In perverse, impetuous agitation, the patch of dry blood cried out to him. He plucked out the blackened surface and clenching it in his hand, carried it to the grave. A dusty ensemble of flowers, bouquets and candles still hesitatingly lay against the mound. Enveloped in a camouflage of white smoke, little flames of blame pointed in his direction.

He turned away from them. The fire's affair with the clothes was finished. A black tower of smoke rising from the ashes suddenly slumped in his direction. Its bias for him made each atom of his hair stand on end and he turned and bolted. The otherwise accommodating distance between the graveyard and the house seemed to have increased on its own. He put on his mask of accomplished task and entered the house.

'I wanted to bring the muddied blood to bury it in the house.' He told Aru secretly.

She admonished him.

'Be discerning.'

He nodded in the dim dusk.

'Go and wash your hands.'

Epilogue

Next day, Ray was on his way home from a nearby market. From the main road, the graveyard appeared like a loose edge of the Christian Compound. Fresh flowers on Yogesh's grave confirmed the contract of death with the living.

His blood was gone but his sweat must tarry in the house, somewhere, holding on to some clothing, some bed linen. Waiting to be curbed by all the washing and cleaning. Over time, he himself would sink into decay and the last vestiges of his odour would ease into the walls and the floors. His memory would be quelled by degenerate routines. Any talk of him would taper quickly to an end like the fading tail of a cunning serpent. In the dusty haze of the provincial road, the memory of such a life would deteriorate from ambiguity to waste. If it could not be extolled then at least it could be paid a homage. If it did not deserve a halo then at least it could be afforded some dignity. If not a pedestal then at least a stone erected in its memory. The words on it should be aflame like his quest. Incandescent during the day. Refulgent during the night. And effulgent in between.

Ray's acceleration of thought stopped. Something blocked his way. It was a night crawler. Its facial features seemed to have been deducted from its face. The mouth seemed to be toothless like a suckling's but when it widened into a smile, the teeth became visible, so black were they due to abuse and neglect!

Unclean in an unconventional way, its grossness was summed up in its glinting eyes, sunk deep within the wanton sockets of its wicked skull. The voice, when it spoke, was like the fading clamor of a gang of rowdy rogues.

'Pehchana nahi?'

Ray shook his head. It gave its name but the vehemence of turbulent truth did not hit Ray until it had finished saying what it had been intending to say for so long.

'Jeevan.'

Ray's memory jangled with cacophonous pealing and he had a vague recollection of a man who years and years ago used to whitewash their Teacher's Row house before Christmas. He smiled at the memory.

'Apke bhai ek gana bahut gaya karte the.'

An aficionado, Ray thought.

'Mera jeevan kora kagaz kora hi reh gaya.'

An unhealthy smirk on its face widened like fever from hell.

'Kora hi reh gaya unka jeevan!'

Ray, unable to even blink, sidestepped the creature quickly and walked away. He would have to tell the story of his brother's life and death. The story of *the second robin.*

****

This novel is the second part of
Death of a Robin
A true account of the events that led to
the death of two individuals.